BLAZERS

Spooked

THE MOST HAUNTED PLACES IN THE UNITED STATES

BY EMILY RAIJ

Consultant:

Barbara J. Fox
Professor Emerita
North Carolina State University

CAPSTONE PRESS
a capstone imprint

Blazers Books are published by Capstone Press,
1710 Roe Crest Drive, North Mankato, Minnesota 56003
www.capstonepub.com

Library of Congress Cataloging-in-Publication Data
Raij, Emily, author.
  The most haunted places in the United States / by Emily Raij.
    pages cm. — (Blazers books. Spooked!)
  Summary: "Describes ten of the most haunted places in the United States"— Provided by publisher.
  Audience: Ages 8-14
  Audience: Grades 4 to 6
  ISBN 978-1-4914-4077-3 (library binding)
  ISBN 978-1-4914-4111-4 (ebook pdf)
 1. Haunted places—United States—Juvenile literature. 2. Ghosts—Juvenile literature. I. Title.
  BF1472.U6R328 2016
  133.1′2—dc23

                              2015001332

Editorial Credits
Anna Butzer, editor; Kyle Grenz, designer; Name, media researcher; Name, production specialist

Photo Credits
Alamy: nik wheeler, 22, 23, Nikreates, 17; AP Images/LAKE CHARLES AMERICAN PRESS/DONNA PRICE, 20, 21 Bridgeman Images/The Battle of Gettysburg, after a 19th century print engraved by John Sartain from a apinting by P.F. Rothermel (litho), American School, (19th century) / Private Collection / Ken Welsh / Bridgeman Images, 14, 15; Corbis: Bettmann, 19; Dreamstime: Tatiana Morozova, cover, Tatiana Morozova, 26, 27; Getty Images: Katrin Solansky, 28, 29; iStockphoto: JohnGollop, (graveyard) 2, 3, 30, 31, 32, SochAnam, cover; Shutterstock: AR Pictures, 24, 25, Bertl123, 8, 9, CAN BALCIOGLU, 1, Christian Mueller, 4, 5, D_D, (paper notes) throughout, (vintage frames and paper) throughout, Natalia Bratslavsky, 6, 7, Sociologas, (old paper strip) throughout, Tueris, (grunge texture) throughout; Wikimedia: Cobra97, 10, 11, Www78, 12, 13

Printed in China by Nordica
0415/CA21500562
032015   008844NORDF15

TABLE OF CONTENTS

SCARY STATES

Scary stories are part of America's history. Some states claim more hauntings than others. Are ghosts real, or could these happenings have natural explanations? Read on and decide for yourself.

THE ALAMO

The Alamo in San Antonio, Texas, was the place of a bloody battle in 1836. For 13 days a small group of Texans fought for freedom from Mexico. Today visitors claim to see **spirits** of dead soldiers walking around this famous place.

spirit—the soul or invisible part of a person that is believed to control thoughts and feelings

ALCATRAZ ISLAND

A famous prison was built on Alcatraz Island near San Francisco, California. Many prisoners died at Alcatraz before the prison closed in 1963. Guards reported moaning, strange smells, cold spots, and the ghosts of **criminals**. **Gangster** Al Capone is the most famous ghost said to haunt Alcatraz.

criminal—someone who commits a crime

gangster—a member of a criminal gang

DID YOU KNOW?

Capone played the banjo in a prison band. Some visitors claim to hear banjo music in the prison's shower room. Could visitors be hearing Al Capone's ghost?

BACHELOR'S GROVE CEMETERY

Bachelor's Grove **Cemetery** is in Bremen Township, Illinois. It seems to be a hot spot for ghostly activity. Visitors report seeing a farmer, a woman carrying a baby, and a two-headed monster.

DID YOU KNOW?

In the 1960s **vandals** began knocking over and spray painting tombstones. Some even broke into the graves, stole bodies, and scattered bones across the cemetery.

vandal—a person who wrecks property

cemetery—a place where dead people are buried

BELL WITCH CAVE

Bell Witch is said to haunt a cave in Adams, Tennessee. The **legend** says the witch began haunting John Bell and his family in 1817. The family heard strange noises and scratching sounds at night. Visitors today report strange shadows and voices.

legend—a story handed down from earlier times; legends are often based on fact, but they are not entirely true

GETTYSBURG

In July 1863, there was a bloody Civil War (1861-1865) battle. Thousands of soldiers were killed in Gettysburg, Pennsylvania. Today visitors report seeing soldiers' spirits lined up on the battlefield and guarding stations.

LALAURIE MANSION

Slaves often disappeared from Madame LaLaurie's mansion in New Orleans, Louisiana, in the 1830s. Neighbors wondered why. After putting out a fire there, firefighters discovered a **torture** chamber. It was filled with dead and suffering slaves. Today screaming ghosts are said to haunt the building.

torture—causing pain to someone

LIZZIE BORDEN HOUSE

Lizzie Borden's parents were murdered on August 4, 1892, in their Massachusetts home. Police thought Lizzie had killed her parents, but a **jury** found her not guilty. Today visitors to the house report flickering lights, crying ghosts, and slamming doors.

jury—a group of people at a trial that decides if someone is guilty of a crime

MYRTLES PLANTATION

The Myrtles Plantation was built in 1796. It is said to be haunted by the ghost of a slave with a chopped-off ear. Today the Louisiana mansion is a bed and breakfast hotel. Visitors report hearing mysterious footsteps and seeing handprints appear on mirrors.

DID YOU KNOW?

Many of the stories about murders and deaths at Myrtles Plantation may not be true. History suggests the owner of the plantation never had slaves.

ROOSEVELT HOLLYWOOD HOTEL

In 1927 the Roosevelt Hotel opened in Hollywood, California. It was a hotel for the rich and famous. Visitors started reporting unexplained events in 1985 after repairs were made. Some people saw ghosts or faces in a mirror.

DID YOU KNOW?

Visitors to the hotel claim to see the ghostly face of Marilyn Monroe. She lived at the hotel for two years at the start of her modeling career.

THE WHITE HOUSE

Is America's most famous house also its most haunted? Many U.S. presidents and first ladies have seen Abraham Lincoln's ghost in the White House. Abigail Adams' ghost has been spotted doing laundry. Dolley Madison may haunt the Rose Garden.

DID YOU KNOW?

Some overnight visitors said the ghost of a soldier carrying a torch tried to set fire to their bed!

WINCHESTER MYSTERY HOUSE

The Winchester family was famous for making rifles. Sarah Winchester believed she was haunted by the ghosts of those killed by the rifles. She built a house in San José, California, to keep the ghosts away. Staircases led to nowhere. Doors opened into walls. Visitors report strange voices and cold spots in the Winchester House.

DID YOU KNOW?

The Winchester Mystery House was under construction for nearly 40 years. Construction stopped when Sarah Winchester died in 1922. At that time, the house was estimated to have 160 rooms!

DO YOU BELIEVE?

We may never know for sure if ghosts and haunted houses exist. Stories and details change over time. Strange events may turn out to be **hoaxes**. Science can explain many mysteries. But it can still be fun to let our scary imaginations run free!

hoax—a trick to make people believe something that is not true

GLOSSARY

cemetery (SEM-uh-ter-ee)—a place where dead people are buried

criminal (KRI-muh-nuhl)—someone who commits a crime

gangster (GANG-stur)—a member of a criminal gang

hoax (HOHKS)—a trick to make people believe something that is not true

jury (JU-ree)—a group of people at a trial that decides if someone is guilty of a crime

legend (LEJ-uhnd)—a story handed down from earlier times; legends are often based on fact, but they are not entirely true

spirit (SPIHR-it)—the soul or invisible part of a person that is believed to control thoughts and feelings

torture (TOR-chur)—causing pain to someone

vandal (VAN-duhl)—a person who wrecks property

violent (VYE-uh-luhnt)—using strong force to do harm

READ MORE

Rajczak, Michael. *Haunted! Gettysburg.* History's Most Haunted. New York: Gareth Stevens, 2014.

Wells, Michele R. *Ghost Stories.* Boys' Life. New York: DK Publishing, Inc., 2012.

Williams, Dinah. *Haunted Hollywood.* Scary Places. New York: Bearport Pub. Co., 2015.

INTERNET SITES

FactHound offers a safe, fun way to find Internet sites related to this book. All of the sites on FactHound have been researched by our staff.

Here's all you do:

Visit *www.facthound.com*

Type in this code: 9781491440773

 **Super-cool stuff!** Check out projects, games and lots more at **www.capstonekids.com**

INDEX